Floella Benjamin OBE is a much loved children's television presenter,
producer and author, who for over 30 years has dedicated her life to
making children happy and campaigning for their well being.
She's written over 20 books including *Coming to England*, her childhood story
and *Skip Across the Ocean*, a delicious book of fun nursery rhymes from around the world.
She is Chancellor of Exeter University. She is married and has two golden children who she adores.

Margaret Chamberlain has illustrated quite a few books about grannies.
Her most famous one is called *The Man Whose Mother Was a Pirate*.
She likes drawing pictures of people dancing, especially grannies.
If Floella hadn't written the bit about the grannies dancing,
Margaret would probably have drawn it anyway. Margaret can't dance yet,
but she is having lessons. She has also illustrated *Tales from Grimm*,
Has Anyone See Jack? and *Look Out, He's Behind You!* for Frances Lincoln.

My Two Grannies

Floella Benjamin
Illustrated by Margaret Chamberlain

F

FRANCES LINCOLN
CHILDREN'S BOOKS

Alvina had two grannies who she loved with all her heart.
They were called Granny Vero and Granny Rose.
   Granny Vero was born on the Caribbean island of Trinidad
and Granny Rose was born in the Yorkshire town of Barnsley.
Now they both lived in the same city as Alvina and her parents.

Granny Vero

Alvina always looked forward to visiting her grannies because she loved hearing the stories they told about when they were little girls.

Alvina, Mum and Dad

Granny Rose

"Tell me about Trinidad again," Alvina begged.

"Don't you ever get tired of hearing the same stories, Alvina?" said Granny Vero.

"Never!" said Alvina.

"When I was your age we would go to the beach, and splash around in the tropical sea," said Granny Vero, with a big smile on her face. "We never wanted to come out of that warm water."

"I would love to do that, Granny V," said Alvina.
"Well, one day I will take you to Trinidad, darlin',"
said Granny Vero. "I promise."

When Alvina saw Granny Rose, she asked,
"Did you swim in the sea all day when you were little?"

"No, luvvie," laughed Granny Rose. "The sea
in Blackpool was much too cold.
But we did play on the
beach all day long and
ride on the donkeys.
We must all go to
Blackpool one day so you
can do that too."

"Oh, yes please!"
said Alvina.

Both grannies loved to play music on their old
record players and Alvina loved listening to it.
Granny Rose played brass band music.

"This music always reminds me of
when we used to go to the park
on Sundays to listen to the local
brass band. On May Day we would
watch the morris dancers fling
their arms in the air and jingle
the bells on their legs as they
twirled around the maypole
to the music."

"Let's try it, Granny R," said Alvina, and they both
fell exhausted into a heap of laughter when they tried
to do the morris dance.

Granny Vero's favourite music was Calypso and steelpan.

"This is what they used to play in Trinidad," Granny Vero explained to Alvina. "It always made me want to dance in the streets at carnival time. Come on Alvina, shake your waist while you dance."

"Like this, Granny V?"
"That's right, darlin'."

One day Alvina's two grannies were at her house
for tea. Alvina's mum said, "It will be our tenth
wedding anniversary next month."

"Why don't the two of you go away
together? I'll be more than happy
to look after Alvina," said Granny Vero.

"No, I will look after her.
She can come and stay with me,"
said Granny Rose.

The two grannies argued and argued about who would look after Alvina. So Alvina said, "Why don't you both stay here and look after me!"

The two grannies frowned at each other but agreed. Yes, they would both look after Alvina.

The day arrived when Alvina's parents were going off on holiday.

"Have a nice time," said Alvina hugging her mum and dad tightly.

"We are going to miss you," said Mum.

"Be a good girl for your grannies," said Dad.

"I will," said Alvina.

"Don't worry, I will look after her," said Granny Vero.
"And so will I," said Granny Rose.

As they waved her parents goodbye,
Alvina said, "Let's play a game."

We can play Dominoes.

We can play Snakes and Ladders.

Alvina did not know which game to play first.
So she said, "Shall we go for a walk?"

Let's go to the park. We can feed the ducks.

We could go to the zoo and see the agouti and the toucan.

At bedtime the two grannies both wanted
to tell Alvina a story.

"How about an Anansi story?" said Granny Vero.

"Or I could tell you the story of
Jack and the Beanstalk," said Granny Rose.

Alvina didn't know which story to choose so she said
she was too tired both hear a story and went to sleep.

The next morning when Alvina got up she had
an idea. She sat down with the two grannies
at the breakfast table.

"Granny V and Granny R, I love the things
you both do for me so why don't you take turns.
Granny V can do everything one day and
Granny R can do everything the next day!"
And that's what happened.

They all played dominoes the way Granny Vero did when she was a girl. Afterwards Granny Vero cooked peas and rice, chicken and plantains with mango flan for pudding.

"This is lovely, Granny V," said Alvina tucking in.

"Mmmm, very nice," said Granny Rose. "You must give me the recipe."

They went to the zoo and saw the agouti
and the toucan – the animals Granny Vero
had seen in the forest as a girl in Trinidad.
"It must have been wonderful to see
those animals in the wild," said Granny Rose.

That night Granny Vero told an exciting Anansi story.

"Anansi would turn himself into a spider whenever he was in trouble," she said.

"Or if he wanted to play a trick," chipped in Alvina, who couldn't help joining in.

"That Anansi sounds crafty," said Granny Rose.

"He is," said Alvina, with eyes wide as saucers.

Alvina gave both her grannies a big hug and fell fast asleep with a smile on her face. The grannies smiled too.

The next day it was Granny Rose's turn. They played snakes and ladders.

"Down the snake I go," said Granny Rose.

"Never mind, Granny R," said Alvina. "You won the last game."

Then they went to the park and Alvina fed the ducks.

"That duck is greedy. It's eating all the bread," laughed Alvina.

"I'll give them some too," said Granny Vero. "This is fun."

Granny Rose cooked steak and kidney pie
with mashed potatoes and carrots and apple pie
for pudding.

"You must show me how to make steak and kidney pie,"
said Granny Vero. "It's delicious."

At bedtime Granny Rose told the story of Jack and the Beanstalk.

"Fee fi fo fum, I smell the blood of an Englishman..."
Alvina and Granny Rose said together.

"I like that part of the story," Alvina said.
"Run Jack, run!"

"Yes, run Jack!" giggled Granny Vero.

Fee fi fo

fum

The two grannies took turns for the rest of
the week to look after Alvina. They really got
to know each other better.

When Alvina's parents came back from holiday
she was excited to see them.
   "Did you have a nice time with your grannies?"
asked Mum.
   "Oh yes," said Alvina. "We had lots of fun.
They both made me feel so special."

"That's because we love you," chirped
the two grannies and they gave her a
great big hug.

MORE PAPERBACKS FROM FRANCES LINCOLN CHILDREN'S BOOKS

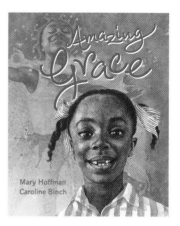

AMAZING GRACE
Mary Hoffman
Illustrated by Caroline Binch

Grace loves to act out stories, so when there's the chance to play a part in Peter Pan, she longs to play Peter. But her classmates say that Peter was a boy, and besides, he wasn't black... With the support of her mother and grandmother, however, Grace soon discovers that if you set your mind to it, you can do anything you want.

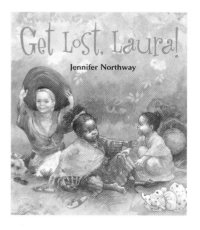

BILLY AND BELLE
Sarah Garland

Billy and Belle can't wait for Mum to have the new baby! When the special day arrives, Dad takes Mum to hospital while Belle is allowed to spend the day with Billy at school. It's pet day, so Billy's hamster comes too. Everything goes to plan – until Belle gets into a spot of trouble over a pet spider!

GET LOST, LAURA!
Jennifer Northway

Lucy and her cousin Alice are trying to play 'Going to the Ball', but Lucy's baby sister just keeps getting in the way. Lucy wishes she would get lost! But when Laura really does go missing, the older girls are desperate to find her. Where can Laura be?

Frances Lincoln titles are available from all good bookshops.
You can also buy books and find out more about your favourite titles, authors and illustrators on our website: www.franceslincoln.com